THE
VISIT

THE
VISIT

WOULD YOU BE READY...?

ADRIAN PLASS

Illustrated by Ben Ecclestone

HarperCollins*Publishers*

HarperCollins*Religious*
Part of HarperCollins*Publishers*
77–85 Fulham Palace Road, London W6 8JB

Text first published in 1987 by Kingsway Publications
as part of the collection *The Final Boundary*

This edition first published in Great Britain in 1999
by HarperCollins*Religious*

Text copyright © 1987, 1999 Adrian Plass
Illustrations copyright © 1999 Ben Ecclestone

1 3 5 7 9 10 8 6 4 2

Adrian Plass and Ben Ecclestone asserts the moral right to be
identified as the author and illustrator of this work

A catalogue record for this book is
available from the British Library

ISBN 0 551 03223 5

Printed and bound in Great Britain by
Bath Press Colour Books, Glasgow

THE
VISIT

1

OUR church used to be very okay. We did all the things that churches do just about as well as they could be done, and we talked about our founder with much reverence and proper gratitude. We said how much we would have liked to meet him when he was around and how much we looked forward to seeing him at some remote time in the future.

The unexpected news that he was going to pay us an extended visit now, in the present, was, to say the least, very disturbing. Confident statements about 'the faith' tended to dry up. People who usually seemed reasonably cheerful looked rather worried. Many of those who had been troubled appeared to brighten considerably.

A man who had always said that 'atonement was a peculiarly Jewish idea' became extremely thoughtful. Someone who had published a pamphlet entitled 'The Real Meaning of the Resurrection Myth' joined the mid-week prayer group and developed an open mind. Desperate folk just counted the days.

Each of us, I suppose, reacted to the news in our own way, but I think the thing we had in common was a feeling that the game (albeit a very sincere and meaningful game for some) was over. No more pretending when he came. He would know.

As for myself, I was looking forward to him coming, as long as it worked out 'all right' – if you know what I mean. I was an organizer, a doer. My job was to keep the life of the church community tidy, make sure that the right people ended up in the right places doing the right things, and I enjoyed being good at it. Granted, I wasn't one of your super-spiritual types, but I smiled and sang with the rest on a Sunday and I seemed to be liked and respected by most folk. God? Well, I suppose my relationship with God was a bit like a marriage without sex – if I'm honest. I'd never got close. But – I worked hard, and I felt I must have earned a small bedsit in heaven, if not a mansion.

So, my job was to organize our founder's visit, make sure it went smoothly, and generally mastermind the whole event. Before long I'd prepared a programme for the day of his arrival and even sorted out who he'd stay with. There was a little wrangling about who that should be. Somebody said it should be a person who was the same at home as they were at church, and someone else said that in that case he'd have to stay in a hotel, but in the end I just chose who it would be and that was that.

My main problem was that I wasn't able to contact him in advance to talk about the arrangements. All I actually knew was that he would arrive for the evening service on a particular Sunday, but I wasn't worried. In my experience, visitors were only too pleased to slot into a clear order of events, and I assumed that he, of all people, wouldn't want to rock somebody else's carefully balanced boat. Isn't it odd when you look back and remember thinking ridiculous thoughts like that? At the time it seemed quite reasonable and I was so used to tying up loose ends (even when there weren't any to tie sometimes), that it never occurred to me that somebody who embodied the very essence and spirit of creativity might, as it were, bring his own loose ends with him.

As the day of the visit drew closer, a sort of mild panic passed through the church. One person said that she felt a visit 'in the flesh' lacked taste and was likely to corrupt her vision of God, another that in his view it was taking things 'too far'. One man, hitherto regarded as being a most saintly character, confessed to an array of quite startling sins, thus becoming, in the eyes of the church, less admirable but far more interesting and approachable. One sweet old lady cornered me one evening in the church room and anxiously asked me the question which probably troubled most of us: 'Is it true that he knows … everything we think?'

I didn't know the answers to questions like that. I just wanted things to go well and looked forward, as I usually did, to the time when it was all over and we could look back and say, 'It really went well!' and, 'Wasn't it worthwhile?' I'm afraid it was to be some time before I learned not to stash experiences safely away in the past before they had a chance to change me.

Anyway, Sunday arrived at last and sure enough – he came.

Now, I know it seems an awful thing to say, but at first it looked as if it was going to be a terrible disappointment – an anticlimax. He wasn't quite what we'd expected. He was rather too … real. His arrival was odd too. I'd planned it to be quite an occasion, and maybe I was wrong, but I was hoping for something in the way of a grand entrance.

Everything was set up, everyone in their places, when we suddenly realized that the man we were waiting for was already there, sitting quietly in the back row. To be honest, I wouldn't have recognized him but, thank goodness, somebody did and suggested he came out to the front.

Well, I was just thinking, 'Great, we can get started now,' but I hadn't even spoken to him when he turned to face the congregation

and said (and you're not going to believe this), 'Has anyone got a sandwich?' Well, a few people laughed, but one elderly lady went straight round the back to the church kitchen and made him a sandwich and a cup of tea, and when she brought them back he sat down on the steps and enjoyed them without any sign of self-consciousness.

I was completely thrown by this. I'd got a copy of the programme in my hand, but when I pulled myself together enough to move towards him, he stood up, turned round and looked at me, and I just couldn't give it to him. I can't describe the look he gave me. It made me want to cry and hit him. That sounds ridiculous, doesn't it, but he made me feel like an idiot, and I admit I felt oddly ashamed as well. But why?

Anyway, he turned to face all the people again and he looked at them as if he was trying to locate a friend in a crowd. He seemed to be searching for a face he knew. Then someone waved to him, and this is where the whole thing just got silly. He ran down the aisle and put his arms round this woman in the fourth row, and she was crying, and he was saying something to her that none of us could hear, and then some other people got up and went over to him until there was quite a little crowd with him in the middle of it.

It was weird. You see, there were people still sitting in their seats, still facing the front, obviously embarrassed and not knowing what to do, while over at the side was this knot of people laughing and crying and making one heck of a noise. Then ... all the noise stopped. Quite suddenly, when he put his hand up, there was absolute silence.

Over at the other side of the church a young fellow was sitting, facing the front, and he seemed to be paralysed. His face was white, his hands were clenched on his knees, and he seemed to be holding himself together by an effort of will. Then there were these two words that seemed to unlock him somehow.

'Don't worry.' That was all. Just, 'Don't worry,' and that young fellow went flying across the church and skidded to a halt on his knees. And then it started all over again – the noise I mean – and then they all went out. They just … went out.

I followed them to the door and I actually managed to catch hold of his coat sleeve. 'Excuse me,' I said, 'I thought we were all going to be together for the service.'

'Of course,' he said and smiled. 'Please come with us.'

I just didn't know what to do.

'But we usually have the service in church.'

'Wouldn't you rather be with me?' he said.

Well, I would have really, but I didn't know where he was going to go. I thought he was going to fit in with us, and he seemed so ... haphazard.

'Where are you going?' I asked.

He looked up and down the road (here's another thing you won't believe), pointed across the street and said, 'What's that pub like?'

I said, 'It's a bit rough really,' and anyway, I knew for a fact that two or three of the people with him wouldn't go into a pub on principle. At least I thought I knew, because they all trailed in there after him; young fellows, maiden aunts, old men – the lot. I was stunned.

I stood by the church door for half an hour and round about half past seven he came out again, and I swear to you he had more people with him when he came out than when he went in. They all swarmed back over the road to the church and he said to me, 'Can we come back in now?'

So they all came back in and sat down. Well, I say sat down – they hung themselves on the backs of pews, sat cross-legged on the floor, draped themselves over the radiators, just anyhow, and he started to talk to them. (All the people who'd stayed in the church when the others went to the pub had gone by then, including the lady he was supposed to be lodging with.)

Now, this is the bit I don't understand. He'd spoiled my service, everything had gone wrong, and he'd made me feel really stupid, but more than anything I wanted to sit down on the floor and listen to him talk – and I got the feeling that he wanted me to.

But I didn't.

I went home.

You know, I haven't cried, not really cried, since I was a little boy, but that night I sat at home and bawled my eyes out. Then, quite suddenly, I knew what to do. I slammed out of the house and ran back to the church. It was so quiet when I got there, I thought they must have all gone, but when I went in there was just him sitting there. He smiled warmly.

'You took your time,' he said. 'I've been waiting for you. I'm staying at your house tonight.'

2

On the day that our founder caused such uproar by returning to the church in person, I nearly lost the chance to be with him, largely because I couldn't accept his refusal to fit in with what I wanted. That got sorted out, and he actually came to live in my house for a time before we found somewhere more suitable.

You'd think I'd learned my lesson, wouldn't you?

I hadn't.

I lived with him, worked with him, saw him do some amazing things, grew to love him even, but I became increasingly infuriated by the way he was distracted by trivial things – or what I saw as trivial things. I still hadn't learned that everything he did always had a reason. Always.

As a result of the anger building up in me, I lost him once again, and this time it was nearly for good.

It happened a few months after his arrival, before he became really well known, and it happened in London. He'd never been there before, but now he'd been asked to speak to a group in the city, so he went, and I went with him. He wasn't always very practical about things like money and tickets and time. My job was simply to make sure he got where he was supposed to be.

We had to go from King's Cross to Victoria on the tube at the end of our journey, and that was difficult enough. I was tired, the train was packed, and when we finally arrived he kept stopping on the platform and staring at people as they crushed around and past him. Each time I managed to sort of tilt him into motion again, but when we neared the foot of the escalator he stopped again, and stood like a rock in the rapids, refusing to budge.

We were late already, and I could feel my patience fading as the knot of anger that seemed to be there all the time nowadays was tightened just a little more. Even so, I'd learned enough about him by then to know that there was simply no shifting him once he'd got a bee in his bonnet, not until he'd done something about it – the right thing. You could always tell when he thought he had done 'the right thing'. His face would relax and he'd smile like a happy child.

When I asked him what was up, he pointed towards the tiled side wall where an old man with one arm was playing a harmonica incredibly badly, and with no great success judging by the pathetic little handful of copper coins lying in a hat on the ground by his feet.

He looked at the old man for a moment, then turned to me with a rather desperate look and said, 'What are we supposed to do?'

'Put some money in the hat,' I said, 'if you want to. But whether you do or don't, hurry please, we must get on!'

He patted the pockets of his jacket. It was a very smart jacket. I'd managed to persuade him to buy one really smart thing to wear for occasions like the one we were heading for.

'I haven't any money,' he said. 'Have you?'

We edged over to the man and dropped something into his cap. At the sight of a note among his little collection of coppers, the old fellow nearly swallowed his mouth organ. Then we let the crowd sweep us forward and soon we were safely wedged on the escalator. I turned amid the din of machinery, and the people's voices, and the fading wail of the harmonica, and looked into his face – to check, I suppose. My heart sank. No relaxed smile. His eyes were full of concern and distraction, and I probably knew what he was going to do even before he did it.

Suddenly, he was gone, burrowing his way back down the escalator until I'd lost sight of him. As he went, I just caught the words: 'I'll see you at the top.'

When I reached the top I was fuming. It was getting really late now, and this was an important meeting we were going to, and he was screwing it up!

I leaned on a ticket machine and waited.

After what seemed like an age, his face slowly emerged over the top of the escalator, beaming satisfaction – and that was okay – but when the rest of him appeared I just felt cold fury. He was wearing a crudely patterned jacket that was ludicrously small for him, and even more absurd, one of the sleeves had been cut off at the armhole and sewn together at the shoulder.

I don't think I even spoke to him, I was so angry. I just marched off and assumed that he wouldn't dare do anything else to hold us up. By the time we got to the hall where he was due to speak I'm afraid I wasn't in very good shape. Don't forget, I didn't understand him as well then as I did later, and it mattered to me terribly what people thought of him – of us – well, all right – me.

I feel terrible when I think of how I felt then, and what I did. As we started to mount the steps towards the big double doors at the top, I looked at this absurd figure who claimed so much, but sometimes

seemed to behave like a weak, stupid person, and to put it bluntly – I was ashamed of him. I deliberately hung back at the bottom of the steps and watched as a little knot of anxious-looking men drew him in. Even from where I was I could see they were looking at him askance in his ridiculous music-hall coat.

The next moment burned itself into my memory. He turned round and looked in my direction, not with anger or annoyance, but with bewilderment and need. He needed his friend with him in those strange surroundings. But by then I'd drawn back, out of sight, into the darkness, and I wasn't there.

It was then that I lost him – not on the escalator. I didn't wait for him to come out that night, and to this day, I don't know how the talk went, or how he got home without a ticket, or anything.

I didn't try to contact him again. I stopped going to the church, and I avoided places where we might have met. I spent the next few months trying to convince myself I was better off without him, but I suppose – secretly – I knew that I'd lost the most important thing I'd ever had. It was the second time I'd walked out on him since we'd met, and I assumed he wouldn't be very interested in seeing me after I'd deserted him when he needed me most.

By the time I did meet him again, he'd become well known all over the country. He'd made a lot of friends and a few rather heavy enemies as well. What with the healings and the big meetings, he was always in the papers or on television, and every time I saw his face a huge grief welled up in me and

18

I had to do something else – quickly. I'd cut myself off because of a stupid jacket and my own foolish pride. I cursed myself over and over again.

One summer morning, when work had taken me back to London, I went for a stroll in the park near my hotel, and there he was, sitting all alone on a bench beside the path. He was gazing at an unopened letter, held at arm's length as though it was about to explode. Everything in me, except the small part that really matters, decided to turn back before he saw me. I didn't. I walked forward and sat down quietly but rigidly beside him, my whole body and mind clenched against rejection. The expression on his face when he turned his head was not one of surprise. It was a mixture of deep pleasure and relief, with not a trace of resentment. I was too near to tears to speak, but he handed me the letter and said, 'I'm afraid this may be bad news. Would you open it and tell me what it says, please?' He turned his head and stared sightlessly over the park, while I opened the letter with rather shaky hands and read it aloud.

It was bad news. One of his closest friends, someone who had welcomed him and shared his vision from the beginning, had died quite suddenly after a massive heart attack.

As I finished reading the letter a strange thing happened. He closed his eyes and sighed from somewhere deep inside him. Simultaneously a breeze moved across the grass and ruffled the leaves on the trees that lined the path. It was as if the natural world was gently sighing in sympathy with him.

Then the moment was past.

He turned back to me and said, 'I'm glad I had time for a little pain, and I'm glad you were here with me. Now...'

'Now?' I said. 'What do you want me to do ... now?'

'Do? I want you to do what you always did. I'm seeing people all the time – every day. I want you to organize me, bully me, help me to help them. You can even … choose my jackets for me if you like.'

I had to ask him. 'Look! Could you just tell me – on that day in the tube, why was it so important for you to go back and swap jackets? It seemed such a pointless gesture. I mean – what use was a jacket with two sleeves to a man with one arm?'

He looked at me steadily for a moment, then smiled shyly. 'None,' he said. 'Actually, I didn't go back to swap jackets, but in the end I felt I had to.'

'Had to?'

His smile broadened. 'You can't leave a man with a new arm and no sleeve to put it in, can you?'

He took the letter and envelope from my hand, stood up, and dropped them deliberately into a litter bin by the seat.

'Are you coming?' he asked, and he stepped out purposefully in the sunshine across the park.

Without a word I got up and followed him, towards the city.

3

I WANTED to see a miracle.

Just one.

One solid, absolutely indisputable, gold-plated miracle, happening before my very eyes.

A small one would do – that would be fine. One ordinary little miracle.

There were two main snags.

First, I didn't want to be the kind of person who needed to see a miracle. I wanted to have the kind of deep, impressive faith that would quietly acknowledge amazing healings, for instance, as mere confirmation of the things I already believed.

Secondly, I kept missing them. In the weeks since our founder had begun his visit to the church, it had soon become clear that he intended to do the same things now as he had done in the distant past, and this included miraculous healings. As usual, people's reactions varied from fascination to hostility, with a strong flavouring of fear. As he himself put it, what a lot of folk really wanted from him was an hour of Paul Daniels, two choruses from 'My Way' and a nice tidy exit through the skylight.

However, the visit continued, and so did the healings.

There were no rules about time and place as far as I could see. It might be a child in the supermarket or an invalid at home or an old man in a pub. The only thing that these incidents had in common (from my point of view) was that I was never quite there to see them.

After the misunderstanding between us when he first arrived, I had begun to learn that formulae and lists and structures were not as important as I thought. He said, though, that I should go on using my talent as an organizer to leave him free to work with people. So I did, and as a result I was busy most of the time, especially as I still had a full-time job as well in those days. It seemed to me that I had always just left the church, or just turned the corner of the street, or just popped out of the pub for a moment, when something miraculous happened in the place where I'd just been. Later, someone would rush up to me excitedly and say, 'You're not going to believe what happened after you left this morning. It was quite incredible...' and so on.

It became more and more difficult to respond to news of this sort with the right kind of enthusiasm. It takes an enormous effort to crinkle your eyes into a Christian smile and say, 'Gosh, how wonderful!' when you actually want to sneer and say, 'Oh yes, and you saw it, didn't you, and I didn't, did I?'

It wasn't, you understand, that I didn't believe in healings. It was just that ... I didn't believe in them. It's hard to explain what I mean. I knew some of the people who were made better. I knew them before they were healed, and I knew them afterwards. Clearly, something amazing had happened and I was duly amazed, and more than ready to defend the truth of their experiences to anybody. It was just that some part of me, a child frightened of being conned by the grown-ups perhaps, wanted to actually see.

Now, you might say to me, 'Why didn't you just tell him how you felt? You could have asked him to give you a shout next time something was about to happen.' And I agree that sounds like a reasonable suggestion. The fact was, though, that he was no easier to predict or pin down now than he had been during his first visit all those years ago. I could never be quite sure how he'd react to questions or comments or people or events. Just as I thought I'd established what he would do in a particular situation, he would do something quite different and even tell me off for saying something that I fondly imagined to be just the sort of supportive comment that he needed.

I remember once, he was sitting with someone in a small back room that we used for interviewing and counselling. I can't recall now who it was, but he or she had just gone through some awful experience and had asked to speak to him privately. I was sitting in the main body of the church, twiddling my thumbs and waiting for him, when a small group of young children clattered through the front door and said they'd come to see 'the nice man'. Well, he always loved being with children, and I thought I knew him well enough to guess the right thing to do, so, in all good faith I told them to go through to the back and find him.

Good faith! Now I'll tell you what I really thought. Two things occurred to me, in the following order.

First, my common sense told me that the children should wait until he had finished what was probably a very delicate and intimate conversation. Right on top of that perfectly reasonable thought came the memory of another occasion when children had wanted to see him and his friends had prevented them. I reached over for a Bible from the pile beside me and leafed through the pages to check the reference. Yes, there it was in black and white. Matthew, chapter nineteen, verse

fourteen: 'Let the little children come to me, and do not hinder them.' A different setting, but the same principle, surely? I wasn't going to get it wrong the way those chaps had. Perhaps I would even earn a word of praise for my thoughtfulness.

Wrong again. He was not pleased. The children reappeared almost immediately. They seemed quite happy, but when he finally joined me, he made it quite clear that, in his view, my first instinct had been the correct one.

My cheeks burn as I remember how at that moment, defensive and flustered, the Bible still open on my knees, I came very close to quoting Scripture to put him back on the straight and narrow. He knew what I was thinking. He always did. He pointed. 'That book,' he said, 'is like the Sabbath. It's made for you, not the other way round.'

It was a point that he made again and again to various people in various ways. He never ceased to be amazed and saddened by the way people seemed to prefer rules and laws and set ways of doing things, to what he once called the 'organized madness of love'. The problem for me was that organized madness could mean doing the sensible thing, or it could mean stepping out and walking on the water. I kept getting it wrong, and that's why I wasn't keen to bring up the subject of miracles. I had an uneasy feeling that he would see straight through my question and produce one of his own. Something like: 'Who do you think that I am?' The strictly honest answer to that question would be: 'I'll tell you when I've seen a miracle.' In other words, I suspected that the root of my problem might be plain, old-fashioned doubt.

The whole thing came to a head when my elderly mother was sent home from hospital after exploratory surgery revealed that she had inoperable cancer. She was given a month to live, and she only had me to spend that month with, so I installed her in a downstairs room and arranged time off work to be with her.

My relationship with my mother had always been an area of pain and guilt for me. As far as I could gather, she had put on disappointment and pessimism like a coat when she was a small child, and she seemed determined to wear that coat to the grave. Her only warm memory, or the only one she ever mentioned to me, was of her father, who died when she was seven. She told me in a rare moment of intimacy that only the memory of his eyes shining with love carried her through the years after his death. She was rejected by her mother, and later made a disastrous early marriage to my father who bullied and neglected both of us until his death some years ago. She seemed to have made a decision early in her life that it was dangerous to be vulnerable and therefore she would never make that mistake again. As a result of this I grew up surrounded by negatives and believing, as children can so easily do, that I had failed in the task of giving my mother the love that she never got from anyone else.

I remember walking into the kitchen after school one day and finding my mother peeling potatoes at the sink. Something about the stubborn misery with which she was performing that ordinary task ripped into me at that moment and, for once, my feelings spilled over into words. Tears of anger and self-pity broke up the image of her resigned figure as I shouted through clenched teeth: 'I'm sorry … I'm sorry, Mum. It's not my fault … it's not … it's not! I'm here too...'

It was the only occasion I can remember her touching me. My vision was still blurred, but I felt the pressure of her hand on my shoulder and, strange as it may seem, that moment of communication, wordless though it was, allowed me to forgive a lot of the discouragement and apparent lack of affection that I suffered in the following years.

And now she was going to die.

As I sat by her bed and studied the grey face, marked with lines of disillusionment and tense with physical pain, I wondered why he hadn't come. I had telephoned places where he might be, places where he had just been, places where he was due to arrive. I had left messages everywhere asking him to come to my house as soon as he could, and still he hadn't come. The thing that hurt me was that he knew anyway. He must know. He knew everything. At any rate, if he was who he said he was, he knew everything.

Realizing that she had passed into real sleep at last, I made my way wearily through to the kitchen to make yet another mug of strong coffee. My head ached with fatigue and worry as I spooned coffee and sugar into the mug and poured boiling water from the kettle. It was as I took my first sip of the hot, sweet liquid that I heard the sound of a man's voice coming from my mother's room. My tired brain whirled helplessly. The doors – front and back – were locked. There was no way in. There was no way that anybody could have got in. No way... Suddenly, calmly, I knew.

I slowly pushed the bedroom door open and there he was, sitting on her bed, holding one of her hands in both of his and saying something very softly to her. I sat down as quietly as I could on the other side of the bed. What was he going to do?

He glanced up at me briefly and smiled, then turned back to my mother. She was awake and gazing straight into his face, her eyes wider than I remembered. I stared, fascinated and moved too deeply for words as her face softened and sweetened, the creases of despair and disappointment re-forming into lines of laughter and happiness. And her eyes had become the eyes of a child who knew beyond question that she was loved and wanted at last. Her lips moved, and as I leaned forwards, I heard her whisper, 'Father, father…'

Then she turned and looked at me in just the way I had always wanted her to. I took the hand she was trying to lift to me and she just said three words: 'All right, son?' It was an apology, a question and a reassurance. It was all I needed. I nodded dumbly.

Then she turned back to him and said, 'I'd like to see you again.'

'You will,' he said, 'soon.'

Then she died, in a room full of peace.

Since then I have seen people made better quite dramatically, but nothing has touched or changed me more than those few minutes at my mother's bedside. I have never seen such love, never seen such healing.

I had seen a miracle.

4

NOBODY had ever confided in me before. Not surprising really – I wasn't the sort of person people tell their secrets to. Recently, though – and especially since our founder's presence on the night of my mother's death – something in me had begun to change. Perhaps I was just beginning to understand that it was not impossible for me to be loved, warts and all. I was somehow less stiff and difficult to approach, I suppose. I was glad about that, but I didn't seem to have any more answers than before, and right now I wished I'd got a few to offer the young man sitting opposite me, as he dabbed a tear away and sniffed miserably.

My visitor's name was Philip. He was about twenty, a good-looking chap, smartly dressed, but nothing out of the ordinary. He wasn't from our church. He belonged to a big, lively fellowship on the other side of town, and at first I couldn't understand why he hadn't gone to one of his own church leaders or elders, or whatever they called them over there. Later, I could see why he hadn't.

It took him a long time to get to the point. He'd seen me, he said, going around with our founder during the last couple of months, and he'd felt that I was … close to him. I'd 'got his ear' as it were. Having established this, he said nothing for some time, just sat hunched in his chair,

gazing at the carpet and breathing very slowly and deeply like one of those athletes you see on television getting ready to do the high jump or the sprint or whatever. Now, I'm not a particularly sensitive sort of fellow, always likely to prompt in the dramatic pause, if you know what I mean, but even I could see that there was no point in pushing him, so I sat back and waited. At last his head lifted, his eyes, frightened but determined, looked straight into mine, and he burst into speech and tears at exactly the same moment. I caught the words as he sobbed them out.

'I'm not normal, I'm not normal!'

Over and over again he repeated the phrase, throwing the words out of him like someone baling a sinking boat. It was some minutes before he was calm enough to take a sip of water and tell me more clearly what he was talking about.

Philip's problem was that he only felt attracted to people of his own sex. He was a homosexual, or 'gay' as such people are called nowadays. He'd never told anyone – family, friends, people in the church, nobody. He'd never had a girlfriend, nor – he added – a boyfriend. I must confess I winced inwardly when he said that, and the 'wince' nearly reached my face. I was the first person he'd ever told, and as I sat facing him, trying to look relaxed, unshocked, wise and defensively heterosexual, it occurred to me that I was just about the last person on earth anyone in his right mind would have chosen for the job. I didn't know any other homosexuals, I didn't know anything about homosexuality, and I'd made a pretty poor job of sorting out my own sexuality, let alone anyone else's. I was quite a bit older than him and I'd never had a girlfriend either. Was I normal?

I was surprised, too, at the strength of the prejudice that must have been lodged in me. When I first understood what he was telling me about himself, certain thoughts popped into my head automatically. I'm not proud of them, but they happened. First, everything in me wanted to gabble something hastily to the effect that I wasn't like him. I was 'normal'. Then, when I was about to move my chair next to his and put my arm round his shoulders, I felt a sudden physical revulsion and fear and stayed where I was. My third, and perhaps most powerful response, was an inner determination to avoid the pain and tumult that was bound to occur if I faced my own sexual problems as he was doing. As I said, they're not very noble reactions, but they only lasted a second, and after a little thought I knew what I should say to Philip.

'Is it that you believe you can't be a Christian and a homosexual? Is that what bothers you most?'

Philip's gaze dropped to the carpet once more.

'I've been in meetings – Bible studies and things. They say it's one of the most … the main … it's in those lists in the Bible. You know, the lists of sins that stop you being – well – being a proper Christian.'

He looked up at me suddenly with the fanatical certainty of one whose convictions had been branded on him by the hot iron of guilt.

'It *is* wrong, you know. The way they talk – they sound so sure, so hard. I could never tell them, but…'

The question – the desperate appeal – in his voice and his eyes quite unnerved me. I leaned my head back and stared at the ceiling, just to escape the intensity of his need. I had no bright ideas at all, no special knowledge or expertise, no rights or wrongs, no thou shalts or thou shalt nots, no specific comfort or criticism. Perhaps I should have been better informed, I don't know. There was only one thing I was sure about. I could best help Philip by being completely honest. I leaned forwards, rested my elbows on my knees, and studied my interlocked fingers as I chose my words carefully.

'Philip, I'd love to be able to say that I know what you ought to do, but I can't because, frankly, I just don't. What I can do, though, is introduce you to him – if that's what you'd like. Mind you, I've absolutely no idea what he'll say or do. I only know that he'll sort it out one way or the other. Whether you'll like what he says…'

An ember of hope flickered to life in his eyes.

'Would he talk to me? I mean, would it matter that I'm … like I am?'

Firm ground at last. I couldn't help smiling.

'It's never mattered that I'm like I am, Philip. I think you ought to give it a try.'

I waited.

'All right,' he said. 'When?'

I set it up for the following day. Philip was to come to our church in the early evening and see him in private for an hour or so. That evening I told our founder how nervous my new young friend was about the meeting. He hardly reacted. 'Wouldn't you be?' That was all he'd say.

The next day Philip arrived early, as I thought he might. I was already there when he walked through the front door. He was terrified. The poor chap was shaking like a leaf. He sat next to me on the front pew and wiped the palms of his hands on immaculately creased trousers.

'He's not here yet, then?'

'Yes, he's round the back waiting for you. We've got a little room there that we use for this sort of thing.'

I could have kicked myself.

'This sort of thing? Do you get a lot of queers coming along for treatment, then?'

There are limits, even to my stupidity. I didn't quite say, 'No, you're the first.' Nearly, but not quite.

'I'm sorry, Philip. I didn't mean that. I just meant—'

'All right, all right … it doesn't matter.'

He stood up.

'I don't think I can do this. What if he says…?

He stared into the distance for a moment, and then, as though someone had silently answered his unfinished question, he walked quickly towards the door that led to the back of the church.

'Through here?'

I nodded. He touched the handle, then turned back to me.

'By the way, I don't know if you think it was silly, but … I dropped a note in to one of our church elders on the way – to tell him what I'm doing. It seemed … I dunno … right somehow.'

I smiled and nodded again. He opened the door, moved forwards, stopped, and turned to me yet again.

'By the way, I'm sorry about getting angry just now – sorry.'

I was getting rather good at smiling and nodding now. I must have come over as an amiable idiot, but at least I wasn't upsetting him. He opened his mouth again as if to say something else, changed his mind and went out, closing the door softly behind him. I flopped back in the pew with relief, expelling air noisily from my lungs. He was in the right place now. I could relax.

I must have dropped off, or at least dozed for a time. A burst of throat-clearing brought me back to full consciousness. A man in a blue suit was standing in front of me. He was very broad, very distinguished looking. His voice was deep and confident.

'I'm sorry to disturb you,' he said. 'My name is Martin Sturgess.'

He smiled and extended his hand, obviously expecting an instant response. When I look blank, I look very, very blank. I got to my feet somehow, and tried to look intelligent.

'I'm sorry, I don't think we've—'

'Philip,' he interrupted. 'I'm one of the elders from Philip's church.'

He held out a folded piece of paper.

'He left this message earlier. I rather wish,' he added reproachfully, 'that he had consulted me before approaching … was it you first?'

'Me – yes, that's right.'

'And then, of course, our founder, whose time is as precious now as it was during his first visit. I can't help thinking…'

My head was aching. It always did ache when I was woken suddenly.

'The thing is, Mr Sturgess, I think Philip was rather nervous about telling you.'

The strong, resonant voice broke in again.

'Scripture is quite clear in this matter. If Philip had confided in me, I would have explained clearly and in detail the course he needed to take.'

He paused, pondering visibly.

'Did you think we would condemn him? Did he say we would condemn him?'

I felt weak and foolish before this big man who spoke with such authority and assurance.

'Well, no, he didn't say that, Mr er … Sturgess. I think he just felt…'

'Yes?'

'Well, look, can I ask you a question?'

'Of course – anything.'

'I just wondered why he didn't confide in you.'

It was his turn to look blank.

'I mean, I wonder what stopped him coming to you. Why didn't he trust anyone in his own church? I mean … why not?'

I trailed off rather lamely. Poor Philip. Of course, like most of us, he did need someone to explain – clearly and in detail – the course he needed to take, but he needed something else as well. He needed—

'Is he with our founder now?' Mr Sturgess interrupted my thoughts.

'Yes, at the back. They'll probably finish soon. Are you going to wait? You're very welcome.'

He stared at me for a moment, then turned and took a few heavily thoughtful steps in the direction of the door. A little way down the centre aisle he stopped and swung round to face me again. His voice rang through the church.

'I am quite sure that when Philip returns in a moment, he will be aware of the seriousness of his position, and the need for proper guidance if he is to remain in the church. I do not condemn him. Scripture

does not condemn him. Scripture condemns the sin, not the sinner. In the last hour, Philip will have learned from the highest possible source that the true Christian no longer needs to sin, and he will need to learn to live in that truth until his faith is evidenced by the changes that take place in him.'

I don't know what I would have said in reply to this speech. Perhaps it was fortunate that Philip chose that moment to come back into the church. He checked for an instant on seeing Martin Sturgess, then walked up and joined us at the front of the church.

'Hello, Martin.'

The young man seemed quite relaxed now.

'Well, Philip?' The elder's voice was charged with anticipation. 'What did he say?'

I must confess I was agog with curiosity myself.

'He said he hoped he'd be here long enough to score a break of fifty on the snooker table.'

He noticed the puzzled frowns on our faces.

'I play a lot of snooker,' he explained.

Sturgess clearly thought this was deliberate flippancy. He took a step forward.

'I don't mean that. You know what I mean. What did he say about your … problem?'

Philip's face became serious. He flushed very slightly.

'Oh yes … that. Well, actually, we only talked about that for a couple of minutes. He said it was very important that we get it sorted out. We're going to talk about it again next week. We're meeting again next week,' he added rather unnecessarily.

'A couple of minutes?' The big man's voice was incredulous. 'What did you talk about for an hour?'

The recollection brought a pleased smile to Philip's face.

'He asked me about myself. What I do, what I'm interested in – that sort of thing. He really seemed to want to know.'

Nobody spoke for a few seconds, then Philip looked at his watch.

'I'm afraid I have to be moving,' he said.

He shook my hand.

'Thanks.'

I think he meant it.

'See you tomorrow, Martin. I'll come round. We'll talk. Okay?'

'Okay,' replied Martin rather weakly, as the buoyant young man headed for the door.

Just before he went out he stopped and called back happily, 'Tell you what – I think he likes me! Cheerio.'

Poor old Martin wasn't looking quite so broad or so confident now. He sat heavily on the end of the nearest pew. After a pause, he looked up at me, and for the first time since we'd met, his smile managed to climb into his eyes.

'I wasn't wrong in what I said, was I?' He spoke very quietly.

I considered.

'Probably not,' I agreed.

'I wasn't right either, was I?'

'No … no, you weren't.'

'I see,' he said ruefully, and with great happiness I realized that he probably did.

5

I STARTED packing at midnight on Saturday. By force of habit I did it as carefully and precisely as I always did everything, but my thoughts were in tatters. I made little whimpering noises as I folded shirts and jumpers, and pushed shoes and slippers into the usual nonexistent gaps. Around one o'clock I fastened the last strap on the last suitcase with hands that trembled slightly but uncontrollably, and stood it in the hall next to the others. For some reason, it seemed crucially important that they should be exactly parallel, and I made minuscule adjustments to each case until I was satisfied.

Pushing the hair back from my forehead with the flat of my hand, I studied the assembled luggage anxiously, hoping that there was something else I needed to do – anything to postpone the moment when guilt and fear would fill the vacuum in my mind yet again. There was nothing left to do though, and no hope of sleep. I turned off the hall light and slid down onto the carpet beside my suitcases. Nobody could reach me now. I had already taken the phone off the hook – its ringing had filled me with dread for days – and if anyone came to the door I just wouldn't open it. I wouldn't so much as move a muscle until dawn, then a taxi to the station, and that would be that.

I had hardly slept for more than a week, and tonight I knew that

I couldn't stand it any more, I just couldn't stand it – the guilt, the despair, the futile attempts to distract myself, the endless cups of coffee in the early hours, and worst of all the flood of graphic scenes involving exposure and humiliation, pumped out remorselessly by my imagination.

There were only two ways I could go. One, meeting the problem head on, was unthinkable – I hadn't the courage. The other was simply to go, just leave and lose myself in the busyness of some other town or city where nobody knew or cared who I was or what I'd done. I just wanted some peace, some sleep.

Most of all, I didn't want to see him again. He was the founder of our church, back for an unexpected visit, and I blamed him for what was happening to me now. He could – should – have known what would happen. Perhaps he didn't care, not about me anyway.

Since his arrival I'd worked flat out to make sure that everything went smoothly on the practical level, and generally speaking I felt I'd done quite well. I'd had to learn a couple of very hard lessons about doing things on his terms instead of mine, but it was unbelievably exciting just watching him in action, and I really had started to feel so much more hopeful and secure in my relationship with him. Recently, though, I'd begun to realize something, and it troubled me constantly.

Other people who were close to him had changed. They were the same people, of course, but they seemed to be happier in some deep, quiet sense. They tended to say less, and when they did speak there was weight and assurance in what they said. They looked as if they felt loved – by him I mean. The simplest way to put it, I suppose, is that they were becoming more and more like him. They maddened me. Their kindness to me made me grit my teeth. I worked as hard, if not harder, than they did. I'd seen them hanging around him, talking, listening, laughing, whispering, often at times when there was work to be done. Nine times out of ten, I would be the one who ended up doing whatever was needed, and after a while I refused offers of help when they did come. Their quiet smiles, their infuriating humility, it was all too much. Still, I did wonder … what about me? Would I ever change? Did he realize just how much work I did, and how much I would have liked to spend more time with him if I could be sure he wanted me? I began to feel bitter – lonely. I worked even harder.

Then, one Friday afternoon, the phone rang as I sat at my desk at home. It was one of the humble smilers, the kindest one. There had been a change of plan. Our founder had decided that he and his closest companions should go away for the weekend on a sort of retreat. I didn't think before replying.

'Fine,' I said briskly. 'When do we start?'

'Well, actually, he's asked me to say that you won't be needed this time. Just relax for a couple of days. You've been working hard.'

An icy calm enveloped me. 'Fine, fine, right, I will. Thanks – enjoy yourselves.'

I lowered the phone slowly onto its rest, and sat for nearly a minute, motionless, my hand still resting on the receiver. 'Won't be needed…'

I rather relished the surge of rebellious anger that swept through me that Friday evening. It made me feel taller, more interesting, more confident. I paced around the house, smacking walls and making aggressive noises to an imaginary audience. Not needed, eh? I'd show them! The anger in me went to my head like wine. In the past I hadn't allowed myself to feel passion of any kind. It frightened me; it was like a bomb that would blow me to pieces if I let it. Now, for the first time, I felt released and hungry for sensation. Suddenly my imaginary audience was not enough. I wanted to go out into the night and feel like a

real person in the real world. I grabbed a coat, checked my money, and swept dramatically out of the front door. As I strode through the darkness, hands deep in my coat pockets, collar turned up round my ears, I felt like a character in a film. Each time a car passed, I imagined the driver catching a glimpse in his headlights of the tight-lipped stranger with the blazing eyes, and wishing, as he moved on towards some dingy

corner of his mediocre existence, that he could be part of the wild, passionate world that this man must inhabit. Who was he, and where was he going?

He was going to the pub, and he was going to get drunk for the first time in his life. Only three pints, but that was two and a half more than I'd ever drunk before. My journey home that night was not easy. The pavement seemed to roll like the sea, and I had to concentrate hard on the problem of balance as successive waves threatened to tip me off my feet.

It was as I stood outside my front door, swaying gently and trying to work out a way to bring the key into contact with the lock, that someone spoke from behind my right shoulder.

'Are you all right, mister er…?'

I turned round, steadied myself, and focused with difficulty on the face of the woman who had spoken. She had forgotten my name, and I had forgotten hers, but I knew who she was. She usually sat in the

fourth row back, next to the wall, in our church, and she lived in one of the bungalows two roads down from me, and she was a bit older than me, and she wasn't married, and I'd sometimes wondered what it would be like to kiss her, but only in weak moments, because it was wrong and … why shouldn't I kiss her? I ached to kiss her. I'd never kissed any woman before, but I was going to now. It would be so sweet … so, so sweet…

She gave a little scream as I put my hands on her shoulders and thrust my face towards her in what must have been a grotesque parody of kisses I had seen on films and television. She pushed my face away with both hands and ran terrified into the road and off in the direction of her home.

The discomfort of what I supposed must be a hangover on the following morning was as nothing compared with the sick terror I felt when I remembered what I'd done to that poor woman. I suppose some people might think it wasn't much, but set against what I claimed to be, appeared to be, and needed to be for the sake of my own self-respect, it was absolute disaster. Drunk and obnoxious, I had tried to sexually assault a member of the church. I, one of his closest associates, I, who had always had so much to say about self-control and discipline and character building. I must have been mad.

The following week was an endless bad dream. I sent notes out to say I was sick, and spent my time roaming the house, looking out of the front windows every now and then, expecting to see a policeman, or a group of stern-faced elders, or the woman herself with a posse of tough male supporters. Nobody came – I ignored the phone when it rang – and the tension increased. I hardly ate, I hardly slept, I wept over the realization that I hadn't a single friend whom I was prepared to trust with my problem. Nobody came, nobody cared – why stay?

Now, as I sat in the darkness of the hall next to my suitcases, waiting for morning, I felt a little better. Soon I would be gone, I would escape, and he couldn't stop me, even if he wanted to.

I must have dozed off, because when I next looked up the first light of dawn was just beginning to whiten the glass panels in the front door. An instant later my body stiffened with apprehension. The silhouette – head and shoulders – of a man had appeared in one of the panels. As slowly and quietly as I could, I rose to my feet, eyes wide with fear, my hands clenching and unclenching with tension. As I turned, intending to retreat to the kitchen, the silence was shattered by an absolute rain of blows on the wooden part of the front door.

I knew it was him.

I clapped my hands over my ears, and shouted over the banging, 'Go away! Go away! I don't want you – please just go away!'

The reply was a single thunderous crash on the door, and in that moment I remembered something.

'You can get in without me opening the door! You did it before – you did it when my mother died. Why don't—'

His voice interrupted me, tense with urgency.

'I can't come in this time unless you let me in.' His words seemed to fill the house. 'You must let me in!'

A further succession of crashes decided me. If he wanted to come in that much, nothing I said was going to make him go away, and I couldn't stand the noise any more. With fumbling fingers, I undid the catch and drew back the bolt. As he put his hand on one of the glass panels to push the door open, panic erupted in me. I didn't want to have to talk to him about what had happened. I couldn't. Desperately, I caught the door as it swung open and tried to slam it back, to shut him out. Instead, to my horror, a glass panel smashed against his outstretched hand, and blood spattered over the inside of the door from a cut at the base of his palm. Aghast, I stumbled back towards the kitchen. He withdrew his injured hand and, pressing it tightly against his chest, closed the door behind him.

There were only two ways for me to go – up the stairs or out through the back door at the other end of the kitchen. I glanced over my shoulder and noticed something very odd. The back door was open – wide open. I knew I had locked and bolted it, but now… There was someone in the kitchen; someone dark and difficult to distinguish was holding the door open for me. For some reason the prospect of passing that, whatever it was, was more terrifying than anything else. I turned and ran up the stairs to my bedroom, pushing the door shut behind me as I went in.

There was no fight left in me, no resistance at all. As I lay curled up on the bed, my face buried in my arms, I was as weak as a kitten, as fearful as a child trapped between nightmares. This time there were

no thunderous blows on the door, he just knocked gently. I heard the door open and close very quietly, then he was in the room and somewhere beside the bed. For several minutes there was silence. I couldn't even hear him breathing. When I finally risked a glance over my shoulder, I saw something I'd never seen before, something that caused the tension and panic to disappear as if by magic. He was weeping, not noisily or dramatically, but with the stillness and concentration that betokens deep feelings. But the thing that caused my heart to leap suddenly inside me, with a shock of joy and total awareness, was the certain knowledge that he was weeping for me. Those tears, still welling up and rolling slowly down his face, were for me. For me!

I swung round and sat on the edge of the bed facing him as he knelt on the carpet, his injured hand pressed on his chest, his eyes, still brimming with tears, fixed steadily on mine. The boss, the king, the top man, was weeping over me, and everything was going to be all right – everything was going to be more than all right. He spoke, quietly but very clearly.

'You didn't understand. I fixed it for you. I fixed it all a long time ago. Getting drunk – the woman – jealousy – everything: they nailed me up for it, I bled for it.' He glanced at his injured hand. 'I'm still bleeding for you.'

There was silence for a few seconds.

'I love you,' he said simply. 'Do you believe me?'

I looked at the red stain spreading over the front of his shirt, at his eyes, red-rimmed, tired, but full of warmth.

'I believe you.' The new happiness in me burst into a desire to do something – anything – for him.

'What do you want me to do? Let's go out and tell everyone what's happened. Or shall I get you a doctor? Oh, no, sorry, you wouldn't need a doctor, would you? Well, what about…?'

He laid a hand on my arm and smiled wearily. 'We'll sort everything out later. Right now, I'll settle for a cup of tea, okay?'

It was okay. At that moment everything was okay.

6

THE last private goodbyes had been said. Today was the final day of our founder's visit, and twenty or thirty of us, those who had been closest to him, were gathered in the church room to hear him speak for the last time. As far as the rest of the world was concerned, he had already gone; this was a sort of close family farewell. Now, thank God, I knew that I was part of that family, and I was more than happy to sit quietly at the back near the door.

I won't tell you what he said to me in our last proper conversation, but I will say it took away most of the dread I'd been feeling about his going.

But how was he going? Where was he going? I didn't know. He didn't seem to hear me when I asked. He just said I should get people together in the church room that evening and put a glass of water next to a chair that wasn't liable to break as soon as he leaned back (he knew that most of our church furniture had seen better days!). I'd done all that, and there he was now, catching my eye over the heads of the others as he leaned back with an expression of mock fear on his face. The chair held, I'm pleased to say, and the buzz of conversation died away gradually until there was a complete hush in the room. For a time he said nothing, just gazed quietly at us with a strange mixture of pleasure and sadness. Finally, he sighed gently, straightened in his chair, and began to speak.

'Today I must go, but before I leave I want to talk to you for a little while about sin. Funny word, "sin", isn't it? Old fashioned somehow. You do all know what sin is, don't you?'

He paused. The stillness that fell over the assembly suggested that we might know what sin was. He went on.

'I certainly know what it is, not least because I had to fight it, just as some of you have fought it – or tried to. You know, during this visit some people have said to me – and I appreciate their honesty – "It's all right for you, you never sinned. You had it easy. You're the boss's son." A sort of divine nepotism, I suppose they mean. Now, the people who say that have got a point in a way. I do love my father so much that it would be agony for me to hurt him, but … I want you to realize something, and I'd like you to explain it to others so that they understand as well. You tell them, when you feel the moment is right.'

His eyes, filled with memory, held us silent and waiting.

'You see, I had the capability, the opportunity, and the power, to do more, to have more, to indulge myself more than anyone who's ever lived or who ever will live. One of your new translations of the Bible says that after I was baptized by my dear cousin, John, I had spirit unlimited. Right! That's exactly what I had. Spirit unlimited – power unlimited. I tell you, I was bursting with it! I went off into that desert like a teenager wobbling away on a huge motorbike that he hasn't learned to control yet. Out there in the wilderness I had to learn how to handle all this power that was surging through me. Out there, where there was nothing, that I faced the fact that I could have anything and everything I wanted: women, money, possessions – the lot. They were all mine for the taking, and don't you believe anyone who says that I wasn't tempted, because I was. I felt every desire for every human indulgence that you do, and I fought it out, in the desert, on my own. That was part of the package, you see – part of the whole arrangement – that I would face it, face it head on, see it for what it was, and choose to turn away from it if it was wrong. Not some of the time, not even most of the time, but on every single solitary occasion.'

His set face relaxed into a smile as an idea occurred to him.

'I'll tell you something that makes me laugh. Those pictures – you must have seen them – of me being tempted during the forty days and forty nights. I'm the cool-looking one with the whiter-than-white robe, dismissing temptation with a rather regal wave of the hand. Obviously you've seen that one.'

He joined in the general laughter, and after a sip of water from the glass beside him, continued quietly and seriously.

'Please don't believe it was like that. I roasted during the day and I froze at night. I was hungry, often thirsty, and always lonely. Most of the time I grovelled on the floor of the desert in a sort of sick daze, and all the time I knew that this incredible power-pack inside me would give me everything I needed or wanted. Warmth, food, companionship of any kind I chose – all available whenever I wanted them, on the spot. I tell you the truth, I knew what one kind of eternity meant in that place. It seemed to go on for ever and ever and ever, but I didn't give in. Shall I tell you why I didn't give in? Shall I tell you what made me strong during those endless days and nights? It was love. Just that. Love.

'I loved my father more than anything in the world. I loved him with all my heart and soul and mind and strength, and I loved you, my

fellow men – even then – as much as I loved myself. You see, my father had said, "Son, do it!" so I did it because I trusted him and I wanted to be obedient. Nevertheless, it took a long time to win that battle completely, but in the end I cracked it. I broke through to a point where I was totally at one with God, wanting only what he wanted, seeing things the way he saw them, and ready to do anything he wanted me to do. Immediately – and this is typical of the way "head office" works – in came the angels with a packet of sandwiches and a change of underwear. You watch out for those angels by the way, they wear some funny disguises sometimes. I saw one the other day with a bottle of meths on Victoria Station, folding his dirty, tattered old wings and trying to find a corner to settle in for the night.'

He was silent for a moment, looking at us as if we should say some-thing at this point, but no one did. Later on at home, I read the last bit of the twenty-fifth chapter of Matthew's Gospel, and began to under-stand it for the first time. He smiled wryly.

'See, I do know a bit about sin. I remember once, when I first came, I was sitting with my twelve lads and talking about the law – the law of Moses, I mean. I think one or two of them were hoping that my message was going to be "anything goes, folks"; a sort of wild, universal party presided over by an amiable old loon in the sky who didn't much care what people got up to. You should have seen their faces as I spelled out the house rules in detail. "Now," I said, "not only can you not kill, you're not allowed to want to kill – to feel that anger that wants to murder. Now, adultery, and the lust that leads to it, are sins of equal value. Now…" and so on, and so on. They weren't happy, I can tell you. "Shifting from ham to ham" I think the expression is. At the end, dear old Peter takes me on one side and says, "I'm afraid I'm out of this, I'm not good enough. Does God really want us to be that good?"

'"Yes," I said, "He does."

'Long pause.

'"Well, I won't make it then, will I?"

'"No," I said, "you won't." Poor Peter looked so downcast at this that I went on to explain something to him, and I'd like to explain the same thing to you now.

'First, the most important thing is to do what God tells you to do. I'd told Peter to follow me, and that's what he was doing. I hadn't said, "Get yourself perfect, and then follow me." Just, "Follow me." The next thing was about the impossibility of ever being good enough for God. It was very important for Peter to know that God's demands are for nothing less than perfection. I wanted him to understand, later on,

what my death meant for him, and how much I loved him, how far I was ready to go to fill the gap between what he was and what he needed to be, if he was ever going to meet the Father face to face. I'd like all of you to understand that as well.

'Let me try to make it clearer. Suppose you and I have known each other for years. You often visit my house; in fact I've given you a key so that you can come and go as you please. Now, over the years you've regularly stolen things from my home, some big, some small, some so trivial as to seem quite unimportant. I've never been to your house – you've never invited me – but one day you're sitting at home when there's a knock at the door. It's me, and I've come to have a show-down with you. Once inside, I start to gather together all the things that belong to me, and I stack them together in the middle of the room, right in front of you. Right through the house I go, opening cupboards, ransacking drawers, reaching under beds, and soon every little thing that you've ever pinched from me is piled on the floor between us. Finally, I reach over and take the biro from your top pocket and add it to the pile, despite your protests that it was borrowed and doesn't really count. So, there we stand by this mountain of stolen goods, and you're pretty troubled by now. What will I do? Call the police? Hit you, perhaps?

'"Did you steal all this stuff from me?"

'There's no point in denying it. "Yes," you mumble. "I'm sorry. What are you going to do?"

'"Forgive you. I just wanted you to know that I knew. Now we can start again."'

He looked searchingly at the faces ranged around the room, then spoke very softly.

'And I know all about each one of you too. I know what you've done, what you want, what hurts you, what you're afraid of. I know what you need. I know you because, in a way that's impossible to explain, I saw – I almost became each of you, during the three hours that I spent dying all those years ago on that hill. You happened in me. You were punished in my body. The time I spent on that cross was a nightmare of congealed darkness and despair, a nightmare filled with selfishness, hate, murder, rape and filth of the most unbelievable kind, as well as apathy, ignorance and all your trivial unkindnesses that never seem to matter at the time. In those three hours I knew what it was to be an addict and a pusher, a torturer and a victim, how it felt to destroy and hurt and damage, and gloat over the agony of others. I knew it, I saw it, I felt it – and in the middle of it all I lost the one I was doing it for. He couldn't bear to look at me and I was so, so alone.'

Someone was crying quietly at the back of the room as he stood up and took a step towards us.

'There's a lot more I'd like to say to you, but I won't now. Just two things. Can I ask you to do something for me? Please, read the book. Get a version that suits you, one you can understand, and I promise you with all my heart that as you read it I'll meet you there, and we'll talk again. The other thing is the most important message I have for you. Look after each other. Forgive each other. Love each other. Don't hurt me. God bless you all and look after you until I'm able to come back again.'

After that he went very quickly. As he passed me he paused, smiled slightly, and said quietly, 'You've changed.'

'Yes.' That was all I could say. Then he was gone through the door into the darkness, and the visit was over.